For Luc and Lily
and in memory of Petelo Kakee
BL

To Ajja, Luka, Dylan
and Madison
MK

ᓇᑦᑎᖅ *nattiq* and the Land of Statues

A Story from the Arctic

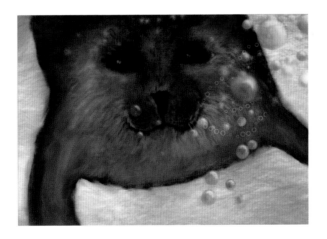

Barbara Landry   Pictures by Martha Kyak

Groundwood Books
House of Anansi Press
Toronto Berkeley

ᓇᑦᑎᖅ *nattiq* calls all the animals to come.

ᓇᓄᖅ *nanuq* shouts out, "What did you see beyond our land?"

ᑑᒑᓕᒃ *tuugaalik*

ᓇᓄᖅ *nanuq*

ᑐᒃᑐ *tuttu*

ᑐᓗᒐᖅ *tulugaq*

ᓇᑦᑎᖅ *nattiq*

ᐊᐃᕕᖅ *aiviq*

ᓇᑦᑎᖅ *nattiq* begins.

"I am swimming through crystal waters,
between gigantic floating mountains of ice,
ᐃᓐᓈᕈᐃᑦ *innaaruit* soaring high above the shore."

"Throughout the darkness of winter
I see the mysterious wonders of the
ᐊᖅᓴᕐᓃᑦ *aqsarniit*."

"In the endless light of summer
the tundra is a blanket of green,
with purples and reds of delicate flowers,
and soft white puffs of ᑲᖑᔾᔭᐃᑦ *kanguujait*."

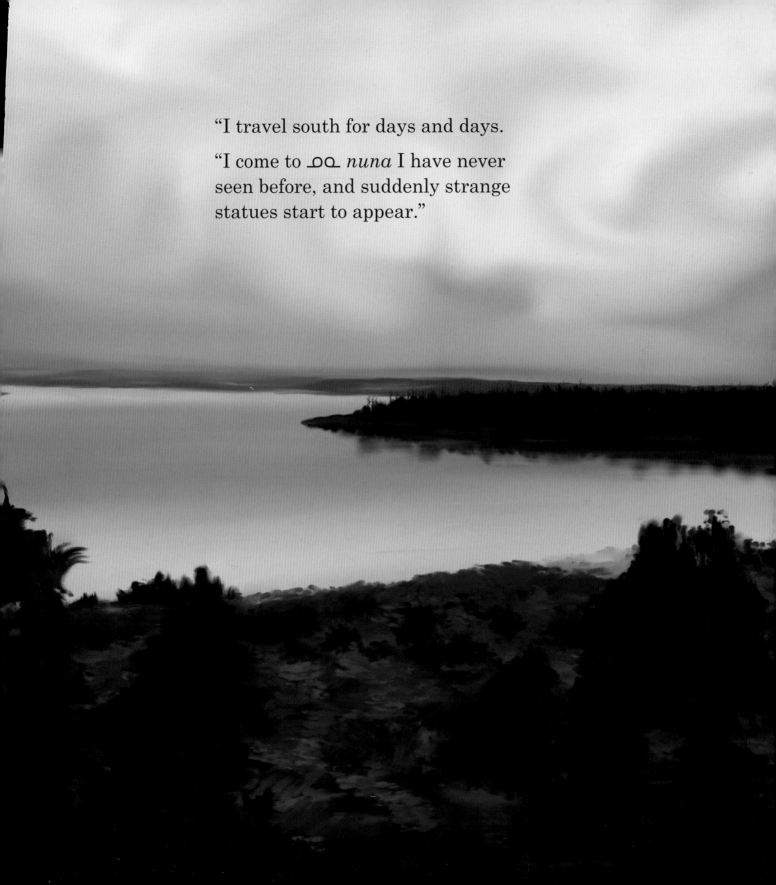

"I travel south for days and days.

"I come to ᓄᓇ *nuna* I have never seen before, and suddenly strange statues start to appear."

"They are small at first,
then bigger and bigger,
rising high into the
ᖅᐃᓚᒃ *qilak*, so high
I cannot see the tops.

"Then I realize the statues
are alive."

"In the ◁⊃⌒ *anuri*, they whisper and nod to one another.

"Dressed in their colorful coats of autumn, they make a beautiful sound in the breeze."

"In winter, when the wind rises, they begin to howl, and in ᔨᓚᕈᔪᒃ *silarujuk* the statues bend and roar.

"Snow and ice swirl around their outstretched limbs."

"In ᐅᐱᕐᖔᖅ *upirngaaq* I hear the songs of birds.

"The statues open their arms to the creatures of the sky."

The animals marvel at this tale.

ᓇᑦᑎᖅ *nattiq* sees their questioning looks.

"They cannot fly. They cannot run or swim. They can never come and visit us."

"But I promised to return each year to tell the giant statues all the wondrous ᐅᓂᒃᑳᖅᑐᐊᑦ *unikkaaqtuat* of our northern land."

GLOSSARY OF INUKTITUT WORDS

ᐊᐃᕕᖅ *aiviq* walrus

ᐊᓄᕆ *anuri* wind

ᐊᖅᓴᕐᓃᑦ *aqsarniit* northern lights

ᐃᓐᓈᕈᐃᑦ *innaaruit* cliffs

ᑲᖑᔾᔭᐃᑦ *kanguujait* Arctic cotton

ᓇᓄᖅ *nanuq* polar bear

ᓇᑦᑎᖅ *nattiq* ringed seal

ᓄᓇ *nuna* land

ᕿᓚᒃ *qilak* sky

ᓯᓚᕈᔪᒃ *silarujuk* bad weather

ᑐᓗᒐᖅ *tulugaq* raven

ᑐᒃᑐ *tuttu* caribou

ᑑᒑᓕᒃ *tuugaalik* narwhal

ᐅᓂᒃᑳᖅᑐᐊᑦ *unikkaaqtuat* traditional stories

ᐅᐱᕐᖔᖅ *upirngaaq* spring

Text copyright © 2020 by Barbara Landry
Illustrations copyright © 2020 by Martha Kyak
Published in Canada and the USA in 2020 by Groundwood Books

The publisher would like to thank Myna Ishulutak for checking the words in Inuktitut.

Groundwood Books / House of Anansi Press
groundwoodbooks.com

We gratefully acknowledge for their financial support of our publishing program the Canada Council for the Arts, the Ontario Arts Council and the Government of Canada.

Library and Archives Canada Cataloguing in Publication
Title: Nattiq and the land of statues : a story from the Arctic / Barbara Landry ; pictures by Martha Kyak.
Names: Landry, Barbara, author. | Kyak, Martha, illustrator.
Description: Includes some Inuktitut syllabic text.
Identifiers: Canadiana (print) 20190153210 |
Canadiana (ebook) 20190153237 | ISBN 9781554988914 (hardcover) |
ISBN 9781554988921 (EPUB) | ISBN 9781773063553 (Kindle)
Classification: LCC PS8623.A514 N38 2020 | DDC jC813/.6—dc23

The illustrations were created digitally.
Design by Michael Solomon
Printed and bound in Malaysia

 Canada Council for the Arts Conseil des Arts du Canada

 ONTARIO ARTS COUNCIL CONSEIL DES ARTS DE L'ONTAR an Ontario government agency un organisme du gouvernement de l'Onta

 With the participation of the Government of Canada Avec la participation du gouvernement du Canada | Canada

 FSC www.fsc.org MIX Paper from responsible sources FSC® C012700